If Cats Could Fly...

But Mel was never content just to be happy. Not satisfied with tagging on to a string of wild geese, trying to imitate their honking noise, and putting them off their migration for several hours, he had to start mucking around with a light aircraft that was making its harmless way towards Thirsk.

He didn't do anything spectacular, that was the awful thing. At first he just flew alongside; but the pilot didn't see him; he was too busy watching the ground. Then Mel pretended to sit on the wing and wash himself, until the pilot noticed him . . .

If Cats could Fly...

Robert Westall

Illustrated by Tony Ross

Mammoth

*For A.J. who wishes that all animals
lived in the peaceable kingdom.*

First published in Great Britain 1990
by Methuen Children's Books Ltd
Published 1992 by Mammoth
Reissued 1998 by Mammoth
an imprint of Egmont Children's Books Ltd
239 Kensington High Street, London W8 6SA

Text copyright © 1990 The Estate of Robert Westall
Illustrations copyright © 1990 Tony Ross

The moral rights of the illustrator have been asserted.

ISBN 0 7497 0936 7

10 9 8 7 6 5 4 3 2

A CIP catalogue record for this title
is available from the British Library

Printed and bound in Great Britain
by Cox & Wyman Ltd, Reading, Berkshire

Contents

Encounters in the Dark

The night they passed their Space exams, Grok and Klek decided to paint the universe red. Or at least drink the bars of Arcturus Four dry. They borrowed Grok's father's new space probe without asking (well, he hadn't said they *couldn't* borrow it).

But after their tenth drink, Arcturus Four seemed *very* dull.

'I'm tired of walking on air,' said Grok.

'Four-dimensional roulette's a drag,' said Klek.

'What's the big match tonight?'

'Arcturus Four against Betelgeuse Eight.'

'Betelgeuse Eight'll wipe them hollow.'

'Let's just take off for *nowhere*,' said Klek.

Grok giggled. He liked the sound of nowhere.

They took off at maximum speed. Since Grok's old man was pretty high-up, he had the fastest thing in space probes. The Universal Police were on to them pretty quickly, and set off in pursuit. But, in three hours, they fell a fatal hour behind.

Only the robo-pilot saved Grok and Klek. It wouldn't let them catch a comet; it wouldn't let them fly through the middle of an exploding nova for a giggle.

'Drag,' said Klek.

'No fun left in the universe.'

'Let's land on the Forbidden Planet,' said Klek, dreamily.

They were pretty far gone by that time. They had crates and crates of stuff in the back, and had finished half of it. They had no idea why the Forbidden Planet was forbidden. Their youthful minds filled it with visions of females in distress waiting to be rescued, horrifying monsters and fiery caverns . . .

'Let's go,' said Grok. And headed for the pretty green and blue planet. Thus adding the crime of planet-breaking to the crime of being drunk in charge of a space probe.

They landed not only safely but neatly on the outskirts of the village of Pulversby. Their robo-pilot deserved the Distinguished Flying Cross that night.

On the outskirts of Pulversby in the Edmonds' house lived another pair of friends. Two cats called Mel and Geoff.

Mel enjoyed playing jokes, like lying in chairs that people were just going to sit in, and rolling over on his back and looking so sweet and helpless that they went and sat somewhere else, much colder and more uncomfortable. Or hanging vertically down the front of the Welsh dresser when people had a mouthful of food

and could be
expected to
spray it all over the
table. Only one thing bothered his
cheerful life. He sincerely wished he
could fly. He was always trying to play
with birds, but just as he was about to touch
them, they flew away. This baffled Mel.

Birds could walk; Mel could walk.

Birds could run; Mel could run.

Birds could go straight up into the air. So
could Mel, but only about a metre. Then he
sort of lost the hang of it and fell back to earth
with a soft thump.

Mel would shake his head so vigorously that
his ears made a rattling noise. Then he could
settle to washing his shoulder, if anyone was
watching. As if he cared nothing for flying,
only for shoulder-washing.

But when no one seemed to
be watching, he practised
flying often. Up and down, up
and down. But he just couldn't
get the trick of it.

'That cat's got the wind in his tail, Alf,' said Mrs Edmonds.

Geoff was quite different, small and golden. He had long since accepted that he couldn't fly. He was a lot brighter than Mel.

What worried Geoff was why things did things. Why squirrels climbed fences vertically, jumped from tree to tree, walked along the tops of high hedges of conifers. He practised all these things himself, and got *quite* good at them (though the watching squirrels thought he made a lousy squirrel and jeered loudly). He never found out the point of doing any of these things, but he went on doing them, hopefully. He also tried to imitate mice, by burrowing into the woodpile. He tried imitating humans by getting into cars and on to buses. It would have got him into a lot of trouble if he hadn't had his name and address on his collar.

None of it made any sense; but Geoff kept on doing things. He somehow knew there was more to life than being a cat . . .

Anyway, the night Grok and Klek landed at the bottom of the garden, Mel and Geoff were curled up together on top of the kitchen cupboard. The top of the kitchen cupboard was a good place to be. It had low wooden walls, for keeping out the draughts and resting

11

your chin on. It was centrally heated by the hot air rising from the gas stove. It had a good view all over the kitchen inside, and all over the garden outside. And neither of the Edmonds' other cats, Kitty or Tigger could bother them, because if *they* tried to scramble up, they could be knocked off again as they hung helplessly to the rim by their front paws. The cupboard top was Mel and Geoff's strong rock and their fortress. Geoff had chosen it after much careful thought. Pity it was full of rusty unwanted tools with sharp edges. But after they had insisted on lying on the tools for a month, Mrs Edmonds had kindly given them an old blanket . . .

Now they pricked up their pointed ears at the space probe's whooshing noise. They watched it land at the bottom of the garden and lie glistening in the moonlight. It looked a good thing to climb up; even to try and fly from.

Then they laid back their pointed ears, as Grok and Klek opened their exit hatch and staggered out.

Now it was as well, that night, that the entire village of Pulversby *were* glued to their telly-screens watching 'EastEnders'. Grok and Klek were good-hearted to a fault, and their mothers loved them dearly but they were four metres

13

high and very thin, with naked silvery skin and rows of pointed knobbles on their heads and down their backs and legs, and eight fingers to each hand. If some horror-writer could have seen them, they would have given him the the entire plot of his next novel.

But only the cats saw them. And to the cats, they looked no more odd than Mr and Mrs Edmonds dressed up for the annual Rotary fancy-dress ball. They just looked *interesting*, a cure for the boredom that all cats suffer from. Mel and Geoff rose, stretched fore and aft, and slipped out of the cat flap to meet them.

'Here come the inhabitants,' said Grok.

'They're very *small*,' said Klek.

'And fancy walking on *four* legs . . . ' said Grok.

'But very friendly.'

'Certainly not hostile,' said Grok as Mel rubbed against the bottom three knobbles of his legs.

'Prook,' said Mel, enthusiastically.

'Meerup,' said Geoff. Then a bad-tempered 'gnaah' meaning, 'I want to be stroked too.'

'Pretty limited vocabulary,' said Grok, bending down to stroke him, and nearly falling over in the drunken attempt. 'But they *feel* nice.'

14

'When you think,' said Klek, giving a wide gesture that indicated the whole universe and nearly made him fall over in turn, 'when you think of some of the horrors that have been discovered in this galaxy...the flame-breathing cannibals of Muk...the strangling scum-clouds of Stu...'

'This lot seem pretty decent, don't they? Primitive...very backward...but...endearing.'

'Let's give them a leg-up,' said Grok. 'Let's push them a bit higher up the ev...ev... evolutionary tree. Let's give them what they *want*.'

'How do we know what they want?'

'Telepathise with them, stupid. You got the top mark in telepathy.'

'I think...I'm too drunk.'

'Oh, let me, for Space sake!' Swaying rather less than Klek, Grok concentrated hard. Finally, he said, 'The black one wants the power of flight.'

'That's easy enough.'

'The other one wants to understand the nature of the universe.'

'Don't look at me. I came bottom in that. Anyway, its head is very small. Do you think there's enough brain in there?'

'Not really. But it's not stupid, either. We

can give it a bit.'

'Right, then, let's get on with it.'

And they did. For it has to be said that in their own way, Grok and Klek were what we would call gods. Very young, very silly young gods. Gods whose appearance would definitely put you off your supper. But gods nonetheless.

'Let's give them *both* the power to fly. Not much fun flying on your own.'

'Done.'

'And . . . I think we'd better give them both the power to think. And telepathise. So they won't be lonely. Thinking by yourself's a terribly lonely business. Drive you mad if you're not used to it. Spesh…spesh…specially if there's only one of you.'

'Right,' said Grok. 'Done.'

The cats went on purring around their legs. They had no idea what was being done to them, but it felt very pleasant, like having your mind stroked.

Just at that point, 'EastEnders' finished. Mrs Edmonds, on her way to make a quick cup of tea, looked out of the kitchen window and saw not only a space probe as big as the parish church squatting on her compost heap, but Grok and Klek halfway up her garden, by the

plastic sundial.

She did the only thing a quick-thinking woman could do. She screamed her head off.

Mr Edmonds came running to the same window.

'Cripes,' he said, 'it's not happening. I don't believe it. It's just not happening.' Then he ran to dial 999 and tell the police what couldn't possibly be happening.

The next-door neighbour, summoned to his back door by Mrs Edmonds' screams, saw Grok and Klek too, yelled, 'The Martians have landed,' and ran for his shotgun.

'Are you sure, dear?' asked his wife. 'It's Leeds University's Rag Week. I'm sure it's just the students up to their pranks.'

'Students four metres high

with *knobbles*?' yelled Mr Brown the neighbour, and opened fire. Missing by many metres, because his hands were shaking so much.

At the bang of the shotgun, Mel and Geoff vanished into the bushes. They'd had many a run-in with chicken farmers.

Grok turned to Klek.

'It seems this planet is also inhabited by another species.'

'Less friendly,' said Klek.

'But also interesting, in their primitive way. Let us retire behind our force fields. And *observe*.'

It is perhaps kinder to the human race not to tell the rest of the story of that night. Except to say it involved a lot of policemen piling out of their Pandas and swearing down their radios, doghandling teams, the police firearms unit in their helicopter, some scientists with a laser which sliced great lumps out of Mr Edmonds' lawn, and five Chieftain tanks summoned from the nearby Royal Armoured Corps tank range at Catterick.

As dawn broke, Grok said to Klek, 'I think we'd better get out of here. There is no reasoning with this species. They are obviously insane. Their minds are a chaos.

I wonder they haven't killed each other off, years ago.'

'Rather have the flame-breathing cannibals of Muk. At least you know where you are with them...'

'And have you noticed our air analyser? There are two hundred and twenty-seven chemicals in this air, and half of them are harmful to all forms of life. That's what the filter contained, when it finally choked up solid. No wonder it's called the Forbidden Planet. Nobody would *want* to come here, if they knew what it was like.'

'They could show it to the Mercutians, as an Awful Example...'

Then they departed in a great flash of light, just before the first TV camera teams reached the spot. Only three perfectly circular depressions remained in Mr Edmonds' garden, each measuring 79.85 centimetres across, and exactly nine metres apart.

There was a total uproar in the gutter press. Some religions foresaw the end of the world. The Police Federation put in for a twenty per cent payrise. But the Ministry of Defence denied everything; the tanks had merely been on night-manoeuvres and got lost in the dark.

On the fringes of Earth's atmosphere, Grok

and Klek were picked up by the Universal Police, and returned to their anxious parents. Grok's space pilot's licence was taken away for five years. Grok's father, Bluk, merely shook his two heads sadly and said, 'Young Arcturians will be young Arcturians.'

His wife shook her two heads and said, 'I only hope they haven't done any lasting harm!'

'If they've done harm, they'll have to go back and undo it,' said Bluk.

2

In the Lair of the Smoking Beast

Geoff wakened at daybreak, in the leaf-filled hole of a hollow tree about a mile away, where they had fled to escape all the banging and swearing. The massive black warmth of Mel, who had lain curled up with him all night, was gone and he felt cold.

But Geoff felt many other things too. He could sense the twittering life all round him; insect-thoughts and bird-thoughts, and the annoyance of a grey squirrel lingering in the top branches, whose drey they had temporarily nicked.

Geoff could also sense the thoughts of Mel. He knew it was Mel because they were fat black cheerful thoughts.

'I can fly . . . I can flyyyyyyy . . . .'

Just at that moment, Mel arrived in the entrance to the hole at too high a speed, slipped and crashed down on Geoff. Geoff spat at him. They were good friends, but not *that* good.

'C'mon,' said Mel. ''S'easy. I'll show you.' He poised himself again, all four paws together and black backside swaying, blocking out the light. 'You just jump, then sort of go on thinking you're jumping.' He sailed away, and

landed in the topmost branches of the tree, in a shower of twigs and leaves, which sent the squirrel into hysterics. 'Come on! Don't be such a scaredy-cat!'

This was a very deep insult. Geoff gathered his dignity and leapt for the ground; only he picked a landing space

24

too far away, that he knew he couldn't possibly reach.

Geoff reached it. Turned, and leapt the impossible leap back to the drey. He reached that too. It *was* easy. The breeze of flight was pleasantly cool round his ears and through his fur. It was *delightful*.

They practised for a long time, Geoff getting neater and neater, and Mel getting wilder and wilder, sending swarms of starlings and sparrows fleeing in all directions, though he didn't catch any. They were too quick in turning; and there being so many of them muddled him.

'Goin' to have a go at those rooks,' Mel said at last.

The rooks were in the top of the highest beech tree. Mel went up among them like a rocket. The rooks weren't all that impressed. They dodged easily, and whereas Mel just hung there, wondering what to do next, the rooks knew exactly what to do. Mel was a menace, and they gave him the same treatment they'd have given to a sparrowhawk, or even a peregrine falcon. They mobbed him; closing in from behind, all nipping with very sharp beaks.

Mel's return was equally rocket-like; with a

bead of bright blood on his right ear, and a rather bent tail.

'Time for breakfast,' said Geoff, before anything worse could happen. 'Jellymeat Whiskas.' Mel liked eating more than anything.

They flew all the way home and landed neatly by the plastic sundial. Unfortunately, Mr Edmonds looked out of the window at that moment and saw them land.

'Our cats can fly,' he said to Mrs Edmonds in amazement.

'Now look,' said Mrs Edmonds, 'I've had *enough*. After last night's carry-on, my nerves

are in shreds. Any more stupid remarks from you, Alf, and I'm just packing my bags and going back to my mother, and you can cook your own breakfast. Is that clear? I *mean* it!' And she waved her grease-dripping cooking slice under his nose menacingly. 'Now,' she added, 'what did you say our cats were doing?'

'Walking up the garden for their breakfast, dear,' said Mr Edmonds humbly. He loved the truth, but not at the expense of cooking his own breakfast and washing his own shirts.

'That's better,' said his wife. 'You get more like your father every day, with his stupid jokes . . . do you want a bit of fried bread?'

Mel and Geoff came in through the cat flap. They both felt the suspicious glare of Mr Edmonds and reckoned they'd have to pull in their ears for a bit. They went up to Mrs Edmonds and stared at her even more soulfully than they normally did at breakfast time.

'Poor things,' said Mrs Edmonds with a sniff. 'Flying indeed!' And gave them extra-large helpings in their saucers, as if they were entitled to damages for libel.

They worked hard at being normal until lunchtime, doing the things they always did, like scratching their ears, and washing between their hind legs, and clawing the arm of Mr

Edmonds' chair, while he was reading the day's football prospects in the *Daily Mail*. After a while, he began to lose belief in his own eyesight. Finally he said, 'I'd better get to the opticians, sharpish!' and went off to watch 'Saturday Afternoon Grandstand'.

Mel rose and stretched. He found behaving well very tiring.

'I'm off flying again.'

'Not again.' Geoff's nerves were a bit on edge with all this newness.

'I mean *really* fly this time. Not messing about from tree to tree like the birds. Flying like an aeroplane. Up in the clouds.'

'Oh heck.' Geoff dearly wanted a lot of time to sit and think the whole thing out. But Mel, alone, had a habit of getting into trouble. 'You'll drive anybody who sees you bananas. We don't want the newspaper reporters here again. We'll get put in a circus, like bears riding bicycles on the telly.'

They were great telly addicts, especially on wet afternoons when Mrs Edmonds was out. Geoff had discovered how to switch it on by treading on the remote-control; pounding away on the buttons while the telly jumped from channel to channel, went brilliant red and blue, then grey, loud, then soft. Their favourite programme was 'One Man and his Dog' when they reached up and swatted the black dogs, as they crawled across the green fields, small as flies.

'If we spread our legs out,' said Mel coaxingly, 'we'll just look like birds. And if we go up very fast . . . when we get high enough, we'll just look like specks in the sky anyway . . . last one to touch a cloud's a scaredy-cat!'

He took off again, like a black rocket. Geoff took off after him, like a rather more reluctant

golden rocket. Two bird-
watchers on Pulversby Hill
spent all the rest of the afternoon
arguing whether they were small ravens or
extremely large quail; it was the end of a
beautiful bird-watching friendship.

But high among the clouds Mel and Geoff
went. There was only one nasty moment, when
Geoff looked down at the distant patchwork of
fields, and felt the whole thing was ridiculous.
The moment he felt ridiculous, he began to
fall . . .

But Mel was down after him in a flash,
grabbing him by the scruff of the neck and
bearing him back aloft. Dear Mel, without a
doubt in his furry black head.

After that, it was pure delight. Pink
clouds, white clouds, yellow clouds, even

pale blue clouds. Cloud tunnels and hills and valleys to shoot down, soar up, tear through. Chase and chase and chase. First Mel chased Geoff, then Geoff chased Mel, then reverse again. It was as near to pure heaven as cats ever get.

But Mel was never content just to be happy. Not satisfied with tagging on to a string of wild geese, trying to imitate their honking noise, and putting them off their migration for several hours, he had to start mucking around with a light aircraft that was making its harmless way towards Thirsk.

He didn't do anything spectacular, that was the awful thing. At first he just flew alongside; but the pilot didn't see him; he was too busy watching the ground. Then Mel pretended to sit on the wing and wash himself, until the pilot noticed him. The pilot's jaw dropped open like the bomb doors of a Lancaster . . . at which point Mel got up on his hind legs, and began to do a tap dance, like they'd often seen Fred Astaire do in the old afternoon black and white films on the telly.

But Mel always went too far. Not content with dancing on the wing, he began to dance on the aeroplane's nose . . . nearer and nearer towards that shining transparent disc of the propeller that Geoff suddenly knew was death . . .

Luckily, it was the tip of his tail that touched it first . . . Mel whizzed back to Geoff like the proverbial scalded cat.

'Only some hairs gone, and a little bit of blood,' Geoff reported. But he felt cold inside. There were invisible dangers in this world, that there had never been in Mr Edmonds' garden . . . Geoff suddenly wished things were still as they had been.

They knew too much now; and yet they didn't know enough.

But Mel was not one to worry for long.

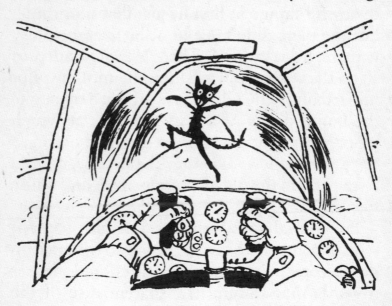

Beyond the light aeroplane, now making a wobbling descent towards Thirsk, he saw an unusual-looking cloud. A dark grey-purple cloud, winding upwards through the other, prettier clouds. And of course he had to fly through that one, too.

Geoff hung back. He didn't like the look of that cloud, somehow. As he got nearer, he didn't like the smell of it, either. It smelt of burning. Even in the speed of his slip-stream, the hair on Geoff's back rose in alarm, and his tail bushed up in threat.

But Mel, without a thought, plunged straight into it. And the next second he was choking, gasping to breathe in more fumes that seared his lungs. Falling over and over, helpless as a shot bird. Down, down, down, he plunged.

And Geoff had to dive after him, holding his own breath, willing Mel to fly, fly, fly.

But still Mel fell, his mouth gasping open and shut, his eyes glazing over, his fur blowing every which way; nearly dead.

And then the air turned clean again. And just in time he heard Geoff's frantic warning, fly, fly, fly.

They landed too hard on a pile of crushed brick, with a paw-stinging thump. Both crouched near the ground, coughing as if they

would cough their lungs up through their mouths. Eyes burning so much they could not see.

'What was it?'

'Great fires. Great smoking beast . . .'

As their eyes cleared, they stared aghast at the great smoking beast, which thrust its many tall thin smoking mouths into the air.

'What is it for?' asked Mel. 'To poison the birds?'

'It is killing more than birds,' said Geoff. 'Kills trees and grass too.'

They gazed doubly aghast at the landscape. The dead grey bare branches of trees stuck up from stagnant lakes, which were covered with swirling patterns of yellow, blue, green. All else was piles of smouldering waste, that gave off foul smells. The grass was long, but brown and dead.

'My mouth is dry. I need a drink,' said Mel. They trotted over to a river that ran close by. But that too was covered with the evil patterns of oil; and in it floated dead fish, bloated white bellies upwards, their scales falling off.

'Do not drink,' said Geoff. 'This is a place of death.'

'What *is* this evil smoking beast? Why do men not kill it?'

'Men *feed* it,' said Geoff, nodding to where huge lorries went grinding up a road, full of brightly coloured chemicals. 'Men serve it.' He nodded again, to where men were crawling all over the beast.

'I do not understand.' Mel grieved with all his generous heart. 'What good are dead trees, dead fish, dead birds? Cannot even be *eaten*.' He looked at the tiny black figures scurrying round the tall chimneys. 'Maybe even kill men . . .'

Geoff shook his head again, until his ears rattled. 'I do not know; but I have smelt that smell before somewhere; I don't know where. Are you ready to fly home now, brother?'

The flight home was long and dreary. At times, Geoff thought Mel was not going to make it. They had to rest many times, so Mel could get his coughing over. But in the end, only a little late for tea, they staggered up the garden path, as Mrs Edmonds came out to look for them.

'You lot look like you've been in the wars,' said Mrs Edmonds.

3

The Big Man in the Silver Car

It was Saturday night, a wet and windy Saturday night that made them glad to be indoors. Everyone was gathered round the blazing fire in the lounge. Mrs Edmonds was knitting, with old Tigger lying stretched out along the back of her chair like a great big tabby scarf. Occasionally, he would sniff at the back of her neck appreciatively, or reach down a massive ponderous paw to dab at the flicking end of her knitting needle. White Kitty was on Mr Edmonds' knee, lying on her back with her paws in the air, and her head dangling down his shins, in total trust. Just occasionally she would raise her head and prook a plaintive plea to have her tummy tickled. Mrs Edmonds called her a floozy.

'It's nice having them all home and safe like this,' said Mrs Edmonds. 'I never stop worrying about them, when they're out.'

'Aye, you get attached,' said Mr Edmonds. 'Comes of never having had any bairns, I suppose.'

'Does that still worry you, Alf?' Mrs Edmonds looked quite desperate for a moment.

'Nay, love,' he said gently. 'I'm quite content with thee and the cats. Cats is a lot less bother than kids.'

Geoff, watching from the hearthrug, envied Tigger and Kitty their innocent peaceful lives; their whole world was the row of gardens behind the cottages. He and Mel could never live in that small world again. Left to himself, he could pretend to, live safe again. But Mel would never be content with that . . . Mel would rove, and get into trouble, as Mel always did. He would have to be looked after.

And the peace of the gardens was only an illusion. Now he was aware of it, the smell of the smoking beast was everywhere; in the curtains, in the carpet, in the very air of the gardens outside. Not strong, not choking, but there just the same.

But somewhere round the house, it was

much stronger than that. If only he could remember where . . .

'We need some more coal, dear,' said Mrs Edmonds hopefully.

'Oh dear,' said Mr Edmonds. 'I don't like disturbing Kitty – she's so comfortable . . . ' It was an old excuse.

Mrs Edmonds sighed and put down her knitting, and picked up the coal scuttle.

Some faint memory made Geoff get up and follow her to the coal-hole. And there, hanging on the back of the coal-hole door, he found his answer. Mr Edmonds' overalls, that he wore to go to work. They *reeked* of the smell of the

smoking beast. Mr Edmonds was a servant of the smoking beast.

'I don't believe it,' protested Mel, on the top of the kitchen cupboard in the silence of the night. 'Mr Edmonds *loves* trees. Look at the time he spends in the garden, watering things! Look at all the plants he brings home! And he loves birds – they always put out scraps for the birds in winter!' Mel moved his paws in great discomfort. 'They are upset when they find a dead bird. He wouldn't want to *poison* things.'

'It is a mystery.' Geoff moved up closer to Mel for comfort.

'Tomorrow we must follow Mr Edmonds,' said Mel.

Geoff sighed. Mel was being just like he'd expected.

But the next day, being Sunday, Mr Edmonds didn't go anywhere. He mowed his lawn, dead-headed his roses. It was not until Monday morning that, wearing the reeking overalls, he set off in the car to work.

They followed, at a height where they might have been mistaken for birds. Mr Edmonds' old red Beetle was easy to pick out, even on the motorway.

'Great road is poison, too,' said Mel, sniffing

gingerly at the smell of lead and carbon monoxide that rose from it.

Straight back to the great smoking beast Mr Edmonds led them; but they were wise, and flew low, under the choking blue-black cloud. They perched on a high roof, watched him park his car and join the stream of workers going inside.

'Why does he do it?' asked Mel.

'Perhaps he is afraid of some bigger man. Like you are afraid of Tigger.' Tigger was boss cat in the Edmonds' house. He had the first choice of where to lie, in the warmest places, free of draughts. Nobody ate from Tigger's saucer, but Tigger ate from everybody else's.

'I'm not scared of Tigger . . .'

Geoff gave him one of his sad disapproving looks.

'Which bigger man?' asked Mel, changing the subject abruptly.

'The man who owns that big car.'

Mel stared at the great silver car that stood apart from the others, as if none of them dared come near it.

'The strongest man would have the biggest car,' said Geoff. 'Watch and see.'

They watched a long long time, coughing occasionally as the fumes reached them. And then their patience was rewarded.

A large man did come out of the works. He walked with a bossy swagger, like Tigger. A smaller man leapt out of the front of the silver car, as he approached it, and ran to open the rear door for the big man, with little bobbings and a lowered head.

'That is the Big Man,' said Geoff, with a triumphant cough. 'The other man is afraid of him.'

'Follow, eh?' Mel took the lead as usual.

The silver car moved off, and the two cats followed at a discreet distance. The silver car went very fast on the motorway, but they were just able to keep up. It swept past all the other cars, as if they weren't there.

'See! All the cars are afraid of the great silver car!' Geoff did so like being right . . .

There was one pleasant thing. As they followed the car, the air got cleaner and cleaner, until it was sweeter than Geoff had ever known it. Hills rose up, bright green and full of large strange animals that they had never seen before. The tops of the hills were brown and purple with bracken and heather.

At last the silver car stopped, in front of a long grey house, with many windows and other great cars parked in front. The great man went inside.

Mel and Geoff perched in the top branches of one of the many trees around, ignoring the rudeness of the local rooks and wondering what to do next. For a long time, nothing moved round the house. Mel got bored. 'Let's go look around?'

After careful thought, Geoff launched himself too. The rooks were getting above themselves; they were missing his tail by a whisker.

They landed in a field with hedges on all sides. The field was full of bright strutting birds, red and blue, with long iridescent tail feathers.

'I'd *like* a feather like that,' said Mel longingly.

'We're here to find out facts,' said Geoff severely. 'Facts are more important than feathers.'

'Not so much fun.' But Mel behaved himself, and put on his most solemn fact-finding expression.

The birds didn't seem at all afraid of them. They were much bigger than Geoff, and nearly as big as Mel. But not nasty like the rooks. They gathered round the curiosities that were Geoff and Mel.

'Men not mad round here?' asked Geoff. 'No smoke? No poison?'

The leading bird looked a bit startled at being addressed; turned its bright beady eye on Geoff. 'Men are our mothers. Keep us warm and dry when young. Feed us every day, until we are strong.'

The other birds chorused together, 'Men are our mothers . . .'

Geoff was dubious. The birds did not seem very bright. 'Aren't you afraid? Of enemies?'

'We have no enemies. If enemies come, men point at them, make big bang. Enemies dead. Some enemies were like *you*. You better push off, before men come. This field is ours.'

Geoff grew more dubious than ever. 'Everything has enemies. Even we have dogs . . .'

'Don't like the sound of the big bangs,' said Mel. 'I don't much fancy being dead. Not much fun when you're dead.'

They flew off gently, and realised they were tired; this flying took it out of you. Not out of your body, but out of your brain. They found a ditch full of tall nettles, turned round and round until they had made a warm nest in the sun, and fell asleep, huddled together as always.

They were wakened by a great shouting and crashing.

'Men,' warned Mel. 'Lots of men with big sticks, beating the nettles.'

'Through the hedge, quick!'

But on the far side, there were more men beating the hedge and nettles with sticks. They had to take refuge down an old rabbit warren.

'What are they trying to kill now – nettles?' asked Mel, rather grumpy from his rude awakening.

'They are making a line – they are driving the big birds across the field.'

Geoff's head was ringing with the panicky thoughts of the beautiful big fat birds. 'Why? Why? Men are our mothers! Why? Why?'

Birds began flying over the far hedge to escape the sticks.

'They are rotten flyers,' said Mel. 'Not much better than hens. I think some of them have never flown before.'

'Perhaps they are driving them into huts, like hens,' said Geoff. 'Let's go and see.'

'Keep low.' Geoff's sleep-filled eyes saw Mel's black backside slide away from him, and lose itself in long grass. He followed him blindly. Nobody could stalk silent and unseen through long grass like Mel. They seemed to go a long cautious way. Then Mel suddenly stopped, so that Geoff blundered into him. 'What?'

'More men. Another line. They are going to make bangs, make dead. I don't like this. Stay low, little brother.'

They heard the shouting and stick-crashing of the first line of men approaching. Then suddenly the sky over the far hedge was full of the big fat beautiful birds, flying very slowly and very badly and in a blind panic, like fat old ladies trapped in a burning building.

'Why, oh, why? Men are our mothers,' came the wail. Wings fluttered, fast and desperate, feathers fell out and floated down gently.

The long line of men raised their guns, and aimed at the birds at point-blank range. There was a volley of bangs so loud that the watching

47

cats crouched deeper, and bent back their ears to close them. What seemed like quick clouds of smoke went up from the barrels of the guns, and hit the fat birds. And the birds just seemed to explode in clouds of feathers. They were no longer flying; they fell down the sky like bloody rags, like thrown-away rubbish.

'All dead,' said Mel and flinched at the presence of so much violent sudden death.

But the worst of it was that most of the falling birds were *not* dead; even the ones who had had a wing blown off. They fluttered helplessly upside down on the grass, or got up and tried to walk, tried to drag their bloody ragged wings behind them, falling down, over and over again. Desperately wanting to escape, to be free, to live. And all the time that terrible crying came from their minds. Why? Why? Why?

Some even managed to hide in bushes; but great dogs came and dragged them out and carried them away, to where men twisted their necks until they were dead.

Another wave of birds came over. Another wave were blown to pieces.

'The massacre of the innocent.' Geoff stirred his front feet in great distress.

'Why don't they fight back?' Mel still had some spirit left.

'What with?'

'I'll show them.' Mel launched himself into the air.

'Keep low, brother,' Geoff managed to warn. 'The men are not shooting low.'

Then Mel was gone, like a black rocket, as the next flurry of helpless fat birds came into view. Right along the line of men Mel flew, a zooming fury from nowhere, a zooming clawing fury that knocked off flat caps, knocked guns sideways, clawed at eyes.

He reached the end of the line and circled back.

'Keep *low*, brother,' warned Geoff. '*Low*.'

Back came the black rocket, along a line of men who were suddenly as terrified and amazed as the poor birds. More caps went flying; more hands were clasped to foreheads.

Mel turned a third time. But now the frightened men were half-expecting him. Guns were levelled . . .

'LOWER!' Just in time Mel dived.

A gun went off.

A man in the line screamed, and held his hands to his face.

Suddenly the whole line of men broke up. All the men dropped their guns and ran to the one that was crying out. He didn't seem at all near dead, but his blue eyes stared wildly out of a mask of blood.

And all the time, overhead, the fat panicky birds were fluttering away to safety.

'One of *them* shot now.' Mel landed back in the long grass. 'See how *they* like it.'

Now the minds of all the men were crying out, 'Why? Why? Why?'

'Time we weren't here, brother.' Geoff could see some of the men pointing at the long grass where he and Mel lay hidden. 'Scarper!'

The cats reached the shelter of the thick hawthorn hedge just in time. Behind them, the long grass was scythed into hay by the blasts of the guns. Then the dogs were sent running in, sniffing.

But by that time, Mel and Geoff were crouched, trembling, high up in a leafy oak. The dogs sniffed in vain.

Finally, the men trailed away, looking angry and discouraged, arguing among themselves about what had attacked them.

'A full-grown buzzard,' said one.

'A black owl,' said another.

'Some eagle out of a zoo,' said a third. 'Pity nobody shot it – it would have looked good, stuffed.'

'You'd only have the RSPB after you, old boy. One hardly dares shoot a thing, these days, but those idiots have you up in court. Snotty-nosed townies – don't understand the life of the countryside at all.'

When the last had gone, Mel rose and stretched luxuriously, and began to lick one front paw. In between his claws.

'Man-skin and man-blood do not taste very

pleasant,' he said. 'But at least we stopped them.'

'Don't fool yourself,' said Geoff gloomily. 'They'll be back tomorrow. Men don't give up that easily.'

'Then we fight again tomorrow . . . '

'Brother, they will be waiting for us. You won't be so lucky again.'

'Well, we come back early — teach fat-birds to fly low.'

Geoff sighed through his nose. He thought Mel was wonderfully brave, but not very bright. 'Do you think these are the only men who are doing it?'

They flew back home wearily. It should have felt like a victory; but it felt more like a defeat. They were so discouraged they only ate half the tea that Mrs Edmonds put down for them.

'Mel and Geoff are off their grub,' said Mrs Edmonds to her husband, later, as they settled down to the evening's telly.

'Is that what's the matter with them? They won't come *near* me. They keep on staring at me, almost human. I don't know what I'm supposed to have done.'

'They're *worse* than bairns,' said Mrs Edmonds. 'At least bairns can tell you what's the matter with them.'

'Aye. If they could speak, I reckon they could tell us a few things . . .'

'They look so miserable, the pair of them, with their ears down like that. You feel so helpless. If they don't cheer up by tomorrow, they're going straight to the vet.'

Mrs Edmonds took Mel on her knee, and Mr Edmonds took Geoff. But they wouldn't settle. The Edmonds couldn't settle to their telly either. It was a most uncomfortable evening.

4

The Choice

The two cats lay awake a long time, that night, staring down the empty moonlit garden.

'I just don't trust humans any more,' said Geoff. 'I think we ought to leave this house.'

Mel shifted uncomfortably on his front paws. 'Oh, these two are all right. We're warm and dry here – we get plenty to eat.'

'So did the fat-birds, until their last day came.'

'These two have been like a father and mother to us . . .'

'That's what the fat-birds said . . .'

'What do you think they're going to do . . . kill us and eat us?' Mel was getting grumpy. He liked his warm place and two meals a day.

Hunting for yourself was fun, but not all the time. It would cut down his time for naps by the fire . . .

'These two are all right because the Big Man isn't around. But suppose the Big Man came and told them to shoot us? And how do you know, that if we flew far enough, we wouldn't find men killing cats and eating them? Because the Big Man told them to?'

Mel stared down the garden; he knew there was no answer to that.

He was still staring, when there was a whooshing noise, and suddenly the space probe, tall as the parish church, was sitting on Mrs Edmonds' compost heap again. The cats watched as two tall silvery figures emerged. This time, they were not staggering, or making a noise. They were walking carefully, on tiptoe, if things four metres tall, with ten toes on each foot, can walk on tiptoe.

The cats ran to greet them gladly; they at least were not *human*.

'Good,' came the familiar voice of Klek who was taking off his driving gloves. 'Here they are, bless them. Now we can undo the harm we have done.'

'Not,' said Grok heavily, 'without their permission. We gave them gifts. It is against the

Universal Law to take them away again; unless they ask us to.'

'Drat the Universal Law. Who's to know?'

'The Universal Police and the Universal Courts. Do you want to be sentenced to Do Good for the rest of your life?'

Klek shuddered. 'No more drinking! No more drag-racing down the Milky Way! No more turning the Universal Courts upside down and leaving them hanging twenty kewks in the air . . . '

'Quite. Now, small brothers, we have an offer to make to you. We can take away your gifts, that are making you outcasts. We can make you happy again, lying in the sun, or by the fire on winter's nights. Without a care in the world.'

Mel looked at Geoff. 'I don't mind stopping *thinking*,' he said. 'But I don't want to stop flying . . . '

Geoff thought a long time. He remembered the happiness . . . but it had been a fool's happiness, where death might have come at any time, without warning, from the hands of those you loved most. He could not get the memory of the dying fat-birds out of his mind.

'No,' he said. 'I will *know*. When my death comes, I will *know* what is killing me.'

Grok sighed. 'I don't blame you. But I'm getting awfully tired of hanging round this dreary little planet. I wish we'd gone to the Betelgeuse game that night. There must be some other answer. I'll have a word with Father Bluk. Bluk will think of a way out. Meanwhile, be very careful, my children. I've got rather fond of you. I'd rather you didn't get your silly little heads blown off . . . ' He bent his great tall body and stroked each of them, with a silver, eight-fingered hand.

The two cats returned, rather sadly, to their strong fortress, and watched the ship take off; in its usual blinding flash of light, that had three inhabitants of Pulversby scrabbling for their bedside phones.

Geoff felt torn in half. All around him was the kitchen, where he had always been so happy. Tomorrow, they would leave it for good. Mr and Mrs Edmonds would never know what had happened to them . . . Mr and Mrs Edmonds would wander the roads and gardens, endlessly calling, endlessly searching, as they had when old Grimalkin went missing . . .

And yet, he and Mel had to go. He had to know all the evil works of the Big Man.

There was no safety anywhere, until he did.

'I wish you would turn your mind off, brother,' said Mel at last. 'We must sleep. It is nearly dawn; nearly time to go and warn the fat-birds.'

The two cats did not wait for breakfast, but flew off into the sunrise. Geoff's heart lifted a little. It was a beautiful morning, only a few white puffy clouds in the sky, and it felt cool and smelt fresher than usual. 'Big smoke less in the dark . . . '

He even started on the weary job of trying to explain things to the fat-birds with a little hope. They found a few, huddled wretchedly under a hedge, who did listen; they were the few survivors of the previous day. Their leader, a huge cock-bird said at the end, 'We will try to remember what you say. But it is hard, when the fear comes . . . '

From the rest, for miles around, it was the same old sickening chorus. 'Men are our mothers . . . '

When the line of men with guns emerged, Mel and Geoff settled at a safe distance. Geoff noticed there were two poorly dressed men, one at each end of the line. Both had shotguns, but they didn't face the first advancing birds. They kept glancing nervously over their shoulders . . .

'Those men are waiting for *you*,' said Geoff to Mel. 'You would not have lived long today, brother.'

Mel shuddered. 'I'm glad I've got you, brother.'

The first birds to be flushed out by the beaters were the survivors of yesterday's massacre. And they *did* remember what they'd

been told. Many flew the other way, over the heads of the beaters, as Geoff had suggested, and escaped entirely. The rest kept low, one even flying into a man's face and, in its terror, splattered wet droppings down his suit before escaping.

'Ruined me damned coat,' said the man petulantly.

'This is rotten sport,' said the Big Man who was next to him. 'These birds have no guts – not flying right at all. I'll speak to the keeper. If he raises such poor-spirited birds next year, I'll sack him.'

But soon, the survivors were gone. And waves of the silly new birds began to arrive, and the slaughter began again . . .

'Enough,' said Mel. 'I feel sick.'

And sadly they flew away.

5

The Prisons

Because they did not know what to do, they flew down into a field of cows. The cows, curious, advanced on them, and stood only a few metres away; staring at the small strangers with dark liquid eyes, and gently drooling grassy liquid from their mouths. They looked extremely fine cows, well-fed, with shining clean coats.

'Men don't seem to have harmed *them* ,' said Mel, ever looking on the bright side. 'They look happy enough.'

Geoff looked at the nearest cow. 'Are you happy?'

The cow looked startled, as the fat-birds had, at having thoughts put in her mind by this totally strange small creature. She backed away rapidly, half-turned to run, and then decided there was nothing to fear from creatures so small, however strange. Finally, her thoughts quietened . . .

Geoff studied her a long time. 'They have taken away her son, and she grieves for him. He was taken from her soon after he was born. For a little while, she heard him calling for her, not far away. He was locked in a little narrow space, where he could not even turn round, or lie down properly. He was very unhappy. Then, after a while, he called no more. She thinks he is dead, now. All her sons have always been taken away from her. She does not know what she has done wrong.'

Geoff glanced at the other cows. 'It has happened to them all. They spend their lives grieving for their children.'

'Let us go. I cannot bear her misery.' Mel took off in a flurry of strangled rage.

They landed next on the roof of a huge long wooden building, and peered down through the ventilators. There was the sound of hundreds of creatures clucking. Inside, under the harsh electric light, they saw rows and rows of tiny boxes, and in each one squatted a hen, nearly filling the box. Some were almost featherless.

'No walking for them; no fluttering of their wings until they die. They lie on wire, which hurts their legs. Their beaks have been taken away. They know nothing except that things should not be this way. Nothing until they die.'

Geoff looked towards where a man emerged, carrying a bundle of dead hens in each hand. He threw them down on a pile of rubbish by the door, as Mrs Edmonds threw ashes into the dustbin.

Mel muttered, 'There is worse, over there, in that small building with the open door. They are throwing living young into a machine that crushes them into pulp . . . *why*?'

'I think they make them into food – for their mothers. It *smells* like food.'

'I cannot believe even men would do that.' Such a weight of grief came from Mel that Geoff told him nothing more.

'Come away from this place of death, brother.'

They roosted miserably in the branches of a sycamore.

At last, Mel spoke, with a feeble shake of his ears.

'How did such wrongness come into the world?'

'I think,' said Geoff, 'it is all to do with *eating*. We cannot all eat grass, like those cows. For men, like us, eating means killing. You have killed many a mouse and a rat, brother. And enjoyed it, without breaking your heart. You lived because the mouse died.'

'Yes. But the mice knew that I was *enemy*. Many have heard me coming and escaped. And the rats knew I was enemy, and they fought. I have had many a painful bite on my nose . . . mice, rats, they have a chance to fight for their lives. They often win. I did not tell the mouse and rat that I was their friend. I did not feed them, look after them, and then kill them when they trusted me . . . '

They were both silent, together, a long time.

Then Mel said, 'I cannot believe that all humans wish this. The people we lived with . . . they *were* kind. They fed the birds in winter. She cried when she found a dead baby squirrel . . . '

Geoff said, 'I have seen things put on their table and eaten. I think now they were pieces of large animals. We have had scraps from them . . . '

'And very tasty, too.'

'I fear we may have eaten that son that the cow was grieving for. Or another son, like him.'

'Are they mad? They cry over a dead squirrel and eat a dead cow.'

'Perhaps they are mad. We know they are poisoning themselves with that smoke. Or perhaps they have been . . .'

'What?'

'Bewitched.'

'Who by?'

'Who are they all afraid of?'

'The Big Man in the silver car?'

Geoff shuddered, and said, 'Yes.'

'Then I shall kill that man,' said Mel. 'And perhaps all will come right.'

'Brother, how can you kill that man? With luck you might scratch his face . . .'

'You will think of a way,' said Mel, with an infinite faith that made Geoff shudder.

6

Attack!

And yet, strangely, a way was shown to them. As they flew back alongside the motorway, an evening mist began to creep up. They kept on flying through denser and denser patches of fog.

'Must go higher. Can't see where I'm going.'

'It doesn't seem to be worrying those cars. They are going faster . . .'

'Mad!'

And then, quite suddenly, there came up through a dense patch of fog a great crashing and squealing of metal that went on and on . . .

'What . . . ?'

'Let's fly down and see.' They circled down

into a misty dew-shrouded field, and crept
back towards the road.

There was a long and terrible heap of
shattered cars; piled up on each other.

'The cars have been fighting,' said Mel.
'They have killed and half-eaten each other.'

'I think there are humans dead, too.'

'When cars fight, their humans die. Brother,
you have given me the idea. I will attack the
great silver car, so it goes mad and fights the
others.'

'I fear you will die yourself . . .'

'I don't care. I do not think I wish to continue
living in this world. And if the Big Man dies . . .
and the world is better . . . you will remember
me, and tell others?'

'I will remember you,' said Geoff with a shudder.

'There he is.'

The silver car was cruising up the motorway towards the works, passing every other car as if it wasn't there.

'Attack from behind.' Mel was leading, as he always did; but Geoff had made up his mind to go with him. If they ended, they would end together. This awful world would be twice as unbearable without Mel.

They had lived together since they met in a pet-shop window as kittens, and Mel had made Geoff his friend, and stopped the other bigger kittens bullying him . . .

'Attack.'

Down they went. Gusts of hot stinking air

flowed up to meet them; strong frightening gusts that plucked at their fur, and tried to throw them in all directions. It was harder for Geoff, because he was so much smaller; but he flew grimly on at Mel's shoulder. The buffeting, the speed was terrible now. He did not know how much longer his mind could hold out, before it cracked into a chaos of fumes and wheels and he was flung under the tyres to be flattened to a pulp like the rabbits they sometimes saw . . .

'Hold on.' He felt Mel's fighting fury mounting. 'Next car.'

And with a thump, Mel flung himself across the car's boot, and hit the car's rear windscreen, paws and claws flailing.

The Big Man in the back had been holding a long black box to his ear. Now he whirled round, his jaws dropping. When he saw the clawing fury that was Mel, he dropped the black box too; his eyes went wide with fear. He shouted something . . .

The man in the front, the frightened slave, turned his head as well. His mouth dropped open too. And then the great silver car swerved suddenly to the right. It hit the metal wall a glancing blow and ran along it; showers of sparks flew up between the car and the wall. And then the man in front regained control, and the car ran on unwrecked.

'Can't hold on!' Geoff felt his mind starting to slip, amidst all the roaring and screeching and stink. In the end, his mind decided it did not want to be a bloody mass flattened on the road. He flung himself upwards and away . . .

Mel, Mel, where was Mel? He could not bear to be in a world without Mel . . .

A fat black thought came into Geoff's mind.

'No good to attack from behind . . . ' He looked up and Mel was floating above him . . . safe . . . 'Attack from in front.' The fat black thought was very very definite.

What was the point of arguing? Geoff was too weary, too lost to argue now. He followed Mel and they overtook the silver car again, with an *enormous* effort. And then they were turning, and Mel was aiming his whole black body at the huge windscreen of the distant silver car.

Somehow, Geoff knew it was the death blow. Death for Mel, death for the frightened driver, death for the man in the back. Death for himself. He had a brief flicker of thought, of regret for the happiness they'd known, the happiness of Saturday nights by the fire, when all the world was right. But it was too late for that. They gathered speed in their death-dive . . .

Every car they passed over, a horrified driver's face looked up. Car after car swerved in terror; brakes went on, feet came off the accelerators . . .

There was a bang and a bang and a bang, as cars slammed into the backs of each other. It sounded like the beating of a gigantic iron drum. It was the strangeness of it that broke

Mel's nerve, and saved his life. He went catapulting into the air, and Geoff after him. They were at five hundred metres, before they knew it. They circled, to get their breaths back, and soothe their whirling minds.

Below, the chaos of wrecked cars in the fast lane grew and grew, a snake of wrecked metal that ate up more cars and more and seemed it would grow longer forever. People scrambling to get out through jammed doors, through broken windows. Then the flashing lights of police cars . . .

'You've killed a lot of cars,' said Geoff at last. 'But not any people. Not even him!'

He was standing on the hard shoulder, shouting wildly at a group of policemen, as if it was their fault. He was gesturing at the sky . . . the policemen were opening and shutting their notebooks, licking their pencils, scratching their heads and not writing anything.

Mel and Geoff landed behind a hedge, and crept closer to see the bitter fun.

'A flying black cat, sir?' said the police sergeant soothingly. 'Your car was attacked by a flying black cat? Clawed at the window . . . you're sure it wasn't a rag of black plastic, sir? Lots of black plastic on motorways . . . caught in the rear windscreen wiper, perhaps? Yes, all

right, sir. It *must* have been a flying black cat.
The ambulance will be here in a minute, sir.
They'll give you a nice little injection, and
that'll help you sleep . . . I'm sure they'll get
you right eventually, sir!'

'I'll *get* him,' said Mel. 'I'll *get* him the next
time.'

'Let's go and get some sleep,' said Geoff. He
just couldn't take any more of the weirdness of
the world.

7

The Torture Chamber

It was three days before the Big Man reappeared. Three long hard days for Mel and Geoff hiding on the sooty roof of the factory with nothing to do but cough at horrible fumes; and try to clean sooty fur that made their tongues sting when they licked it.

But he turned up at last, in an even bigger and shinier silver car than before. He went inside, but didn't stay long.

'Follow.'

They followed at a safe height, in a new direction. Finally, the car turned in at a gate in a high barbed-wire fence. There were uniformed men at the gate, who checked the car carefully before they let it through. Beyond

the barbed-wire fence was another, and another. In between were beautiful green trees and parkland. And right in the middle of the parkland was a white building, with a flat roof.

'Is this his stronghold?'

'We shall see!'

Again they landed, and peered through open ventilators. Again, cages. Bigger cleaner cages now, but still cages. Full of white rats and white rabbits, and small gentle-looking monkeys and even dogs.

'There are some of our own people down there.' Mel grew very agitated. 'Some are in agony. Men cut them open, then they swell up and hurt, hurt all the time. I cannot stand this. We *must* do something!'

Silently they stared down at the captive cats, who sat and lay with weary baffled patience, some with flaps of skin raised on their heads, and coiling wires inserted.

'Too many men,' said Geoff. He watched the white-coated men going to and fro, opening the cages to clean them out, or interfere with the animals inside. He noted carefully how the men lifted the catches to open the doors. 'But men go home at dark like Mr Edmonds. Watch telly, drink lager. Then . . . '

Geoff noted how the men turned the handles

of the building's main doors. 'Go down, open cages, open doors . . . ' He was not at all sure it would work. But they had to do something; they had to *try*.

They settled down to wait for the setting sun.

At first, it went well. As the sun set, they watched the building empty, the men drive away. Darkness settled over the parkland. Soon, the long aisles of the building were empty, the electric lights dimmed to a twilight. Only in the parkland a few men patrolled, talking to tiny boxes held in their hands.

'What about them?' asked Mel. 'How do we get past them?'

'Easy in the dark, for small things. Out there, under trees, small things quicker than men. Let's go.'

They slipped through the open ventilators, and glided to the smooth polished floor.

There was a tremendous hubbub among the animals. A thousand shining dark eyes watched them come. A thousand ears pricked. Who? What? Why?

'We are friends. Come to set you free. Be silent, or the men will come.' This last was to the dogs who were starting to bark. They needed no second telling.

Such excitement. The monkeys, even those strapped down with wires in their heads, began to beat on the floor of their cages with their hands. The rats awoke from long boredom, and leapt from one side of their cages to the other. Even the placid rabbits twitched their ears and noses furiously.

Mel and Geoff trotted from cage to cage. Standing up on their hind legs, they pushed up the catches with strong shoves of their noses, until their noses were sore; then they used their paws.

Furry bodies dropped to the floor, and ran to

and fro with the joy of being free. There came a strong smell of animal droppings, dropped in their excitement.

'Be still, brothers, or the men will come.'

Every animal was still.

Geoff left the strapped-down cats until last. He felt a great wretchedness in approaching them. He was afraid of harming them further.

'You want be-free?'

The first cat looked at him. 'Want be-free even if I die for it. Chew straps, brother. Chew wires . . . '

There were many willing teeth to chew straps and wires. Soon the cats were free too, short lengths of wire trailing from their heads. But free.

'Now door.' Mel went towards it.

All the animals gathered in a crowd around him, as he reached up and dragged at the long shining handle. The door began to swing open, and the smell of the night wind, full of the scents of water, leaf and freedom, came to all their trembling nostrils. Once out in the dark . . .

The sound of ringing bells was terrible. They were like great terrible metal giants, screaming with rage. All the animals cowered, close to the shining floor, paralysed with fear.

Outside, blinding lights came on, illuminating every twig and blade of grass with white brilliance. Then brilliant lights inside, too. Geoff despaired, crouched with the others.

Men came running, dozens of men with metal helmets on their heads, gabbling into the boxes held in their hands, and swinging long heavy sticks in their other hands.

'Animal Rights loonies, breaking in,' gabbled the men into their boxes. 'Main doors. Do you read me, police control?'

All the animals round Mel and Geoff fled. Many were so afraid they fled back into their own prisons and crouched in tight balls on the sawdust, with flattened ears and closed eyes, waiting for the worst.

Mel and Geoff were left standing alone.

'Grab 'em,' shouted a man, and reached for Mel.

There was a terrible hiss, and the man swore and leapt back, sucking a bleeding hand. Another man flailed at Mel with his long stick. And another, and another. Mel dodged and twisted and struck back, but it was only a matter of time before a fatal blow hit him.

Geoff had never been a fighting cat, like Mel. He was a thinking cat, who saw the end of things only too well. But when your best and only friend . . .

Geoff took off, and came back like nothing so much as an outraged golden hornet. He battered and clawed again and again at helmets and hands and sticks and faces.

Mel managed to stagger to his feet.

'*FLY, YOU FOOL.*'

Mel got the idea in a dazed sort of way, and flew, rather like a bee that has taken too much pollen aboard on a hot summer day.

But he flew.

They gained a ledge near the ceiling, and stared down sadly at the wreckage of their plan.

And the men stared up, open-mouthed at the

very idea that cats could fly. And there were several men in white coats among the security-men now. Men whose faces were filled with evil wonder.

'Cats that can *fly*,' they yelled at each other. 'The phenomena of levitation. We must catch them, probe them . . . '

'Test them; examine their brains.'

'If all else fails, vivisect them, dissect them.'

'We are on the very frontiers of science . . . '

'Trap them. Close the ventilators . . . '

'Bring the gun with the anaesthetic darts...'

'Shoot them down . . . '

'We shall be famous. Nobel prizes. The very frontiers of science.'

There was a whining grinding sound. Too late, Mel and Geoff turned to see the ventilators grinding shut behind them.

Geoff knew there was no hope. They were trapped. They might fly and dodge for hours. But their end was certain. Into the cages. Up with flaps of their skin. On with the electrodes. For the frontiers of science . . .

8

Exodus

It was at this point that the true frontiers of science turned up outside.

Grok and Klek.

Now it is one thing to investigate a frontier of science that is small and furry and helpless.

But quite another to investigate a frontier of science that is four metres tall, with two heads and bright knobbles all down its silver back. That reaches to open *your* door with an eight-fingered hand.

Suddenly, the men in white coats no longer wanted Nobel Prizes. They wanted the Fuzz, the SAS, the Royal Armoured Corps. Above all, they wanted their mums.

They all vanished in search of these, as fast as

their legs would carry them, screaming their heads off.

'Odd race,' said Grok. 'No sense of hospitality.'

'Not even any manners,' said Klek. 'Really! You'd think we were hideous. Who are they to criticise, single-headed apes?'

Mel and Geoff purred with pleasure at seeing their old friends. They flew down from the ledge, and rubbed against Grok and Klek's lower knobbles, purring with great delight.

Grok and Klek stroked them.

'We've come to sort you lot out,' said Grok.

'You're upsetting the Universal Police with your antics. They've been watching you, you know. From up there. They watch *everybody*.' Klek said this with much feeling.

'You've got a choice,' said Grok. 'We either make you back as you were, or you'll have to come with us. Where you can't do any more harm.'

Geoff thought hard. He remembered, with a fleeting sadness, their happy life with the Edmonds, before it all began to change. Then he remembered the poison, and the cow and her son, and all the helpless captives.

'We'll come with you,' he said, 'if there's no poisons or prisons.'

'No poisons or prisons,' said Grok.

'I swear it, by the two heads of my mother,' said Klek. Which was such a terrible oath that even Geoff was convinced.

Then Mel looked round the lab; at all the other animals, who were creeping out of their prisons again, hoping wistfully to share a little of the general kindness that was going on. Their eyes were on him . . .

'And if we can bring all our friends,' he said.

The animals went into the space probe two by two. There were female cats among the captives. At first, all the she-cats fancied the great hero Mel. But in the end a black and white female came up to Geoff. 'There's not much of you,' she said, 'but you smell all right to me.' Which Geoff wisely took as a compliment.

'They're talking about kittens already,' said Mel darkly. 'I'm not sure I want to commit myself. I enjoy my free-wheeling lifestyle.'

Then they all took off in a great flash of light, and none was ever seen on this earth again.

From a hundred miles, they looked down with mild curiosity at the green and blue orb floating in space.

'It's pretty from here,' said Geoff. 'You can't see the smoke.'

'I wonder how long they've got before they finally poison everything?' said Mel.

'About twenty more years, if they don't change their ways,' Grok told him, looking up from the controls.

'I hope Mr and Mrs Edmonds will be all right,' said Mel sadly. 'And all the birds they feed in winter.'

Grok looked round the cabin. It was lucky

they were large creatures, and had a large cabin. Fifty cats had occupied one of their bunks, and fifty smallish dogs the other. Rabbits were lolloping all over the floor, dropping droppings. The white rats had taken up position in every darkened nook and cranny. And the monkeys were starting to pull levers and turn wheels . . .

'This is going to pin their ears back, on Arcturus Four,' said Grok with glee. 'We're going to have more fun than that time we hid all the balls before the match against Alpha Centauri Seven . . . '

'It will be strange not to be the only species on our planet any more. Less lonely, somehow . . . ' said Klek.

'I wonder if they've got telly where we're going?' said Mel.

And then they were just a dwindling point of light in the vastness of space.

Robert Westall

THE CHRISTMAS SPIRIT

A ghost and a cat arrive for the holidays in this pair of Christmas stories.

In *The Christmas Cat*, a girl's miserable holiday at her uncle's vicarage is saved by the appearance of an unruly neighbour and an abandoned, pregnant cat. In *The Christmas Ghost*, a boy has a hair-raising Christmas Eve encounter with a ghost at the factory where his father works — a ghost who must convey a desperate message.

It is only by convincing the adults around them to believe – in them or in other people – that the two young protagonists can save the spirit of Christmas.

Two classic Christmas stories by Robert Westall, winner of the Smarties Prize, the Guardian Children's Fiction Award and twice winner of the Carnegie Medal.

Robert Westall

THE NIGHT MARE

Miss Crimond was sitting in Dad's chair which had once been Grandpa's chair; and Billy hated her.

To Billy and all the families who rented her houses in Back Tennyson Street, Miss Crimond was the arch enemy.

Billy and his gang declare war. In between the street cricket and football, they go into battle. There is the firework down the chimney that fills the house with soot; the deliveries, not requested by Miss Crimond, of coal she has to pay for and manure that comes up to her eyes.

But Billly's campaign has unexpected consequences when he sees the night mare, the horse of his dreams, and finds out what a special and clever man his grandpa had been. . . .